WHAT CAN YOU SEE?

PAUL ROGERS

ILLUSTRATED BY
KAZUKO

A Doubleday Book for Young Readers

Tilly and Bouncer, out looking for fun,
Find a balloon in the middle of town.
Tilly goes up. But Bouncer stays down.
All Tilly takes is her telescope.

Over the gardens and rooftops and roads
Tilly's balloon lifts her gently away.
As she looks down on the busy, bright day,
What does she spy with her telescope?

A bird on a chimney, a clock on a tower,
A factory's smoke that melts in the air—
Tilly spots each of them. Can you see where?
But she can't see Bouncer. Can you?

So many buildings! Too many to count!
Cars of all colors, so shiny, so small.
Tilly glides quietly, queen of it all.
What does she spy with her telescope?

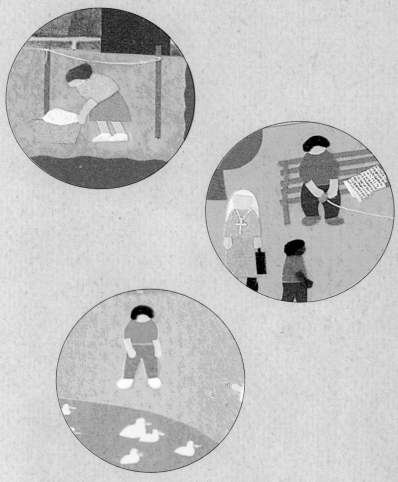

Clothes on a clothesline, dogs playing tag,
A man in the park with a child on his knee,
A blue-and-red kite caught up in a tree.
But she can't see Bouncer. Can you?

On past a building site teeming with men.
Diggers and bulldozers claw at the ground,
A bright yellow crane swings slowly around.
What does she spy with her telescope?

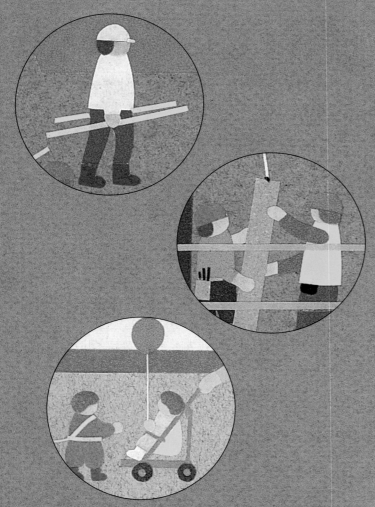

A man with a telephone pressed to his ear,
A child in a stroller, a flag on a pole,
A man up a ladder, a man in a hole.
But she can't see Bouncer. Can you?

Higher and higher, as light as a bird,
Tilly looks down on a world without noise.
Trains full of people seem tiny as toys.
What does she spy with her telescope?

A rusty old lawn mower lost in the grass,
A baby, a lady with flowers in her hand,
A boy on a bike at a newspaper stand.
But she can't see Bouncer. Can you?

Way down below her she spots a parade:
Bandsmen in uniform, crowds all around,
So far away that she can't hear a sound.
What does she spy with her telescope?

A flash of gold cymbals, a juggler on stilts,
A leopard-skin jacket, a tiger-striped cat,
A tall, waving feather on somebody's hat.
But she can't see Bouncer. Can you?

Over the highway, past the canal,
Town turns to country, gray becomes green.
So many things now too small to be seen!
What does she spy with her telescope?

A boy with a fishing rod under a bridge,
A boat with a bright orange swirl on its side,
A horse in a meadow, a boy on a slide.
But she can't see Bouncer. Can you?

Over the hedgerows, the farmyards and fields.
Sheep on their shadows, cows in the shade,
Over a duckpond the farmer has made.
What does she spy with her telescope?

A tractor, a doghouse, pigs in a pen,
A party of rabbits, a scarecrow, a nest,
A man with a backpack who's taking a rest.
But she can't see Bouncer. Can you?

On beyond villages—then, up ahead,
There lie the beach and the dreamy blue sea!
Sunbathers everywhere, happy and free.
What does she spy with her telescope?

A picnic, a fishing net, gulls on a ledge,
A blue-and-white beach ball, a pink rubber ring,
A beautiful sandcastle fit for a king.
But she can't see Bouncer. Can you?

Now the balloon's getting lower and lower.
Tilly holds tight as it swoops to the ground,
Lands in the grass with a whispering sound.
There's someone to meet her. Guess who!